Very Veggie Murder

Book Three

in

Papa Pacelli's

Pizzeria Series

By

Patti Benning

Author's Note: On the next page, you'll find out how to access all of my books easily, as well as locate books by best-selling author, Summer Prescott. I'd love to hear your thoughts on my books, the storylines, and anything else that you'd like to comment on – reader feedback is very important to me. Please see the following page for my publisher's contact information. If you'd like to be on her list of "folks to contact" with updates, release and sales notifications, etc…just shoot her an email and let her know. Thanks for reading!

Also…

…if you're looking for more great reads, from me and Summer, check out the Summer Prescott Publishing Book Catalog:

http://summerprescottbooks.com/book-catalog/ for some truly delicious stories.

Contact Info for Summer Prescott Publishing:

Twitter: @summerprescott1

Blog and Book Catalog: http://summerprescottbooks.com

Email: summer.prescott.cozies@gmail.com

And...look up The Summer Prescott Fan Page on Facebook – let's be friends!

If you're an author and are interested in publishing with Summer Prescott Books – please send Summer an email and she'll send you submission guidelines.

TABLE OF CONTENTS

VERY VEGGIE

MURDER

Book Three in Papa Pacelli's Pizzeria Series

CHAPTER ONE

"Hold on, Bunny. I want to zip up," Eleanora Pacelli said to her little papillon. The dog paused at the end of the leash and looked back at her, puzzled as to why the exhilarating hunt for leaves had paused.

Ellie slipped the loop at the end of the leash around her wrist and fiddled with the zipper on her jacket, taking a couple of tries to get it all the way up without snagging. Once it was zipped, she felt warmer immediately. The steady breeze coming from the ocean was becoming icy, a sure sign that the weather was changing—as if the colorful leaves on the trees weren't enough of a hint. In just a few short weeks, Kittiport, Maine, would see its first snowfall of the season. She wasn't looking forward to it. The hot, sunny days of late summer already seemed like a distant memory.

She began walking again, the little black-and-white dog ranging out ahead of her as far as the leash would allow. Leaves blew across the road in front of them, and Bunny growled playfully at those who dared come too close. Ellie smiled, enjoying the sight of her beloved friend enjoying herself so much. The dog always brightened up her day, just by being her happy, exuberant, furry self.

After a few more minutes, Ellie decided it was time to head back. It was getting close to the time that she would have to head into work, and she wanted to make sure that she would be able to take Marlowe out of her cage first. The macaw was not happy with her at the moment. Her cage, which had been moved next to the stairs in the foyer after Ellie's grandfather passed away, was back in the study for now, and the bird was definitely not a fan of being cut off from all of the activity.

I wish I could just explain it to her, Ellie thought, idly kicking at a stone on the pavement as she followed the bouncing dog back toward her grandmother's house. *She doesn't understand that Uncle Toby, Aunt Kathy, and Darlene are only going to be here for another week and a half, then things will go back to normal.* When her family members had first arrived, the bird had greeted them by screaming loudly, unhappy with the intruders in her home. When she had continued the earsplitting squawks whenever one of the guests walked through the front door, Ellie had made the decision to move her, figuring it would be better for everyone involved. Marlowe had been giving her the stinkeye ever since.

"At least *you* like them," she said to her dog. The papillon was simply thrilled with the houseguests. With Ellie's aunt, uncle, and cousin around, the pooch never ran out of people to feed her treats.

A strong gust of wind made her shiver and pull her hood up. Something cracked in the woods, making her jump. A man had been killed in those woods, part of a state park, just a few weeks ago, and even though the killer had been caught, Ellie still regarded the dark spaces between the trees with suspicion. It would be a while, she knew, before the memories from the previous weeks faded. At least the full house didn't afford her much time to dwell on the past.

It took her longer than normal to get all of her stuff together and leave the house that afternoon. The second guest bedroom upstairs had been taken over by Darlene, Ellie's cousin, who seemed to have taken to heart Ellie's pro forma invitation to make herself at home. She had unpacked everything she had brought, and was terrible at putting things back in their place when she was done using them. The bathroom was a disaster, but even worse, their laundry had somehow managed to get mixed together. By the time Ellie found the shirt that she was looking for on her cousin's bed, she was late to work and could only be grateful that her relatives had gone out on the *Eleanora* for the day; otherwise, who knew how long it would have taken her to get out of the house?

"It's not that I don't enjoy visiting with them," Ellie said to a bored-looking Clara a few hours later. "We're having a big family dinner tomorrow night, and I'm looking forward to it." The young woman was leaning against the counter propped on one elbow, flipping half-heartedly through an old magazine with her other hand. It was a slow day at the pizzeria, and both women had already finished all of the chores that they normally had to do. With Jacob out on a delivery, the two women were alone in the empty restaurant.

"It's just that Nonna and I have a certain way we do things. We both enjoy the peace and quiet, and we clean up after ourselves as we go. Darlene and her parents talk so loudly *all* the time, even when other people in the house are still sleeping. And they leave the dishes in the sink and only clean them in the evening. It drives me crazy. I like having a clean sink, but I don't want to spend all of my time doing *their* dishes."

"Uh-huh," her employee said, slowly flipping another page.

"I mean, they're nice enough people," Ellie continued. "I actually really enjoy spending time with Darlene, and hope we stay in touch after this. We seem to have a lot in common. She's about my age and married, but still very independent."

"How are they related to you, again?" the young woman asked, her eyes still on the magazine.

14

"Kathy is my aunt. My father's sister," she explained.

"Ah." Clara turned another page. "Cool."

Ellie's lips twitched. "Sorry. I know I'm probably boring you."

"Nah, it's fine. I know what it's like to have family drive you crazy. I had to live with mine for eighteen years, and I've got four brothers. At least you've only got another, what, two weeks?"

"Ten days," the older woman said. "And I *am* glad I'm getting to spend some time with them, despite my complaints. I suppose I'm just not used to living with people. It's one thing to live with Nonna, but three other people? It's tough."

Maybe it's a good thing I ended up not getting married. Kenneth would probably have driven me insane, she thought, suddenly depressed. *Am I fated to spend my life as a spinster?*

CHAPTER TWO

By the time the sun set the next night, Ann Pacelli's house was full of people and the promising smell of dinner. Ellie cracked open the oven and eyed the two pizzas inside, which she and Darlene had spent the last forty minutes making.

"Not long now," she said. "How's the salad coming, Aunt Kathy?"

"Just about ready. Do you want me to mix the croutons in, or leave them on the side?"

"They might get soggy if they're mixed in. I'd leave them out," Ellie suggested. "Thanks for showing me how to make croutons at home, by the way. I never knew how easy it was. I doubt I'll ever buy them from the store again."

"For someone who runs a restaurant, you don't seem to have a lot of experience in the kitchen." Her aunt blushed and quickly added,

"No offense. Ma told me your pizzas are to die for, and that's what counts when you're running a pizzeria, right?"

Ellie just laughed. "Honestly, I hardly cooked at all before I moved back here. I was always too busy. I'm really just getting the hang of pizzas—if they're good, the credit should go to Papa. I just follow his recipes."

"Yeah, Dad always had a way in the kitchen," Kathy said, smiling. "I think Ma was a bit jealous. They were pretty traditional while we were growing up, and she thought that she should be the one cooking our meals. She's a good cook, don't get me wrong, but Dad really was something special. He had a passion for it."

I wish I had gotten a chance to get to know him better, Ellie thought as she grabbed a pair of oven mitts. *He sounds like a wonderful man, but I hardly have any memories of him. He was always so busy back when I lived here during high school, and besides, that was decades ago. Maybe I'll be able to get Nonna to tell me more about him later. If I'm taking over his restaurant, I really should know* something *about the man other than that he loved to cook and he owned a boat. I also need to remember to ask her for a picture of him that I can blow up and put on the wall. She's mentioned it before, and I really need to remind her.*

Resolved, she pulled the pizzas out of the oven and placed the pans on a pair of cooling racks on the counter. As if by magic, Darlene appeared at the kitchen doorway.

"Are they done?" her cousin asked.

"Sure are. I think they turned out wonderfully." She stepped back from the pizza pans. "Take a look."

"Ooh, delicious. Thanks for letting me help, Ellie. It's been a long time since I've made homemade pizza."

"Of course. It was fun to do it together." She smiled at her cousin. They hadn't seen each other in years, but it was easy to recognize the teenage girl she had known in the grown woman in front of her. There was the same spark of mischief in her eyes.

The doorbell rang, and Darlene's head whipped around. "That must be Danny. I'll go get it," she said over her shoulder as she hurried out of the kitchen. "You go ahead and put the pizzas on the table. I'll tell Dad and Nonna that dinner's ready."

Ellie smiled to herself as she picked up the familiar curved blade and began cutting the pizzas with confident rocking motions. Danny was an old friend of Darlene's, and her cousin had been beside herself with excitement when she managed to get into contact with him and invite him to dinner with the family. The pizzeria manager was eager to meet this man that she had heard so much about. Darlene had practically talked her ear off while they were making the pizzas, regaling her with stories about summer camp and lazy summers spent fishing with the cute neighbor boy. If Danny turned out to be half as interesting as her cousin said he was, Ellie would be impressed.

"I just wanted to thank everyone for welcoming me," Danny said once they were all seated. "It was wonderful to get that call from Darlene. It's been a few years, hasn't it?"

"It has," Aunt Kathy said. "But you're always welcome at our table."

"Thanks," he replied with a smile. "That means a lot."

"I'm glad you could come," Darlene said. "I want to hear all about your new store, but first, let's dig in. These pizzas look too good to wait."

At that the family began helping themselves to slices of pizza and salad. Ellie took one slice from each of the pizzas, and helped herself to a serving of greens and homemade croutons, her gaze flicking back to the man sitting across from her all the while. He was handsome and well-groomed, with straw-colored hair and just the hint of some stubble on his cheeks. He seemed quick to laugh, and so far, had been nothing but courteous to her and her family. He seemed to know Aunt Kathy and Uncle Toby quite well, and she couldn't help but wonder how. Had she ever met him during her childhood? If so, it had been so long ago that all memory of their meeting was gone.

"Nice pizzas, you two," Uncle Toby said. "The vegetarian one is your doing, Darlene? It's not half bad."

"They're both delicious," Nonna agreed, dabbing at her mouth with her napkin. "Ellie, you've really got some of your grandfather's skill when it comes to making pizza."

"Thanks, Nonna," she told her grandmother with a smile. "I do my best."

"Though," the elderly woman added with a mischievous twinkle in her eye, "he usually made proper pizzas at home for dinner. None of this thick-crust stuff."

Ellie rolled her eyes. Her lips twitched up in a smile; their different tastes in crust thickness had become a running joke between the two of them. The pizzeria manager was of the firm opinion that thicker crust was better, with the best, of course, being Chicago deep dish from the Windy City itself. Nonna, on the other hand, shared the misguided taste of the majority of New Englanders and preferred thin-crust pizzas.

"Variety is the spice of life," she told her grandmother. "Darlene's vegetarian pizza is thin crust, so you can just eat that."

"A woman shouldn't have to choose between having meat on her pizza and having a proper crust," Nonna grumbled good-naturedly. "What do you think, Danny? Which pizza do you like better?"

"Oh, both are great. I'm not a picky guy," he said, chuckling. "I'm just happy to have good food and good company."

"Ellie runs Papa Pacelli's now," Darlene told him. "You should stop in the next time you're in town. She's done a lot with the place."

"Oh, really?" He turned his gaze to Ellie, impressed. "I didn't know that. I'll be sure to check it out. How long have you been there?"

"Not very long. About two months, maybe," she told him. "Have you ever been there?"

"Oh, a couple of times," he said. "I live in Benton Harbor, and don't have the time to come up to Kittiport much anymore."

Benton Harbor was the next town down the coast, about a half-hour's drive from the center of Kittiport. Ellie was sure that she had been there at some point in her childhood—it was on the way to

Portland, after all—but she couldn't remember much about the town.

"What do you do there?" she asked. "Darlene said something about you having a new store?"

"Danny opened a shoe store there earlier this year," her cousin said. "He sent me an invitation to his grand opening, but I couldn't make it. I've been dying to hear all about it though."

Both woman looked expectantly toward Danny, who laughed. "It really isn't that interesting. I've been thinking about starting my own business for a while. Commuting down to Portland every day just wasn't cutting it for me. I had been messing around with ideas for a couple of years, when one day I realized that the obvious answer was staring me in the face. Benton Harbor didn't have a shoe store."

Ellie raised her eyebrows. Coming from Chicago, she was used to having any sort of store she wanted just minutes away. How could there not be a single shoe store in a whole town?

"Everyone just went down to Portland or came to Kittiport for shoes," he said. "And of course there are a few stores in town that sell work boots, secondhand shoes, and winter boots, but none of them have very big selections. I decided to open a dedicated shoe

23

store." He shrugged. "It's been pretty successful. I'm never going to get rich from selling shoes in Benton Harbor, but it's a fun adventure, and much better than driving down to Portland every day to work in an office."

"I think that's really neat," Darlene said. "Isn't it, Ellie? Maybe you two should team up and do some sort of... pizza and shoes promotion."

"Pizza and shoes?" the pizzeria manager said, chuckling. "I'm not sure those two things go together very well." She turned to Danny. "But feel free to stop by the pizzeria any time and hang up an advertisement for your shoe store and leave business cards if you want. I'm always happy to support other local businesses."

"You do the same," he said, smiling at her. "We small business owners have got to stick together."

CHAPTER THREE

The rest of the meal was pleasant, though once talk shifted away from business, Ellie didn't have much to say. She listened instead, and discovered that Danny used to live near Darlene when they were younger. Ellie's cousin had been homeschooled, but the two had gone to summer camp together, and Uncle Toby had even gotten Danny his first job at the paper mill that his father-in-law had run. Even Nonna knew him; she had met him a few times at mill events that she had attended years ago with her husband.

When the conversation turned more reminiscent after dessert, Ellie began to feel a bit left out. She didn't share any memories past her teen years with these people. It was evident that they were having a good time, and she decided that they would probably enjoy their conversation just as much without her.

She got up during a lull in one of her aunt's stories about some family gathering that had happened years ago and excused herself to the study, telling them that she had to finish up an order form for the pizzeria. It was a half-truth; she didn't have to get the order in until noon the next day, but it wouldn't hurt to get it done early. Besides, she wanted to spend some time with Marlowe. The parrot had been alone in the study for most of the day, and deserved some attention and treats before bed.

Bunny followed her out of the dining room and down the hall, pausing to glance back just once when a roar of laughter sounded from behind them. Ellie couldn't help but smile. The little dog so obviously wanted to be back in the room with the food, but loyally stuck by her side anyway.

"You're a good girl," Ellie told her. "I've got treats in the study. I'll give you a couple, just don't let Marlowe catch you eating them. She thinks that all food is hers."

The papillon at her heels, she slipped into the study and shut the door quietly behind her. Marlowe greeted them with a squawk and raised her wings up, a clear sign that she wanted to get out of her cage. Ellie paused by the desk to grab a few treats out of the dish and drop them onto Bunny's bed before walking over to the large metal bird cage and opening the door.

"Come on out, sweetie. I'm sorry you've been locked in here all alone for so long."

27

She held out her arm, which the parrot stepped onto from her perch. Ellie pulled her out of the cage, the bird's scaly feet gripping her arm tightly. Once free of the bars, Marlowe stretched her impressive green and blue wings out, then tilted her head to the side and eyed the woman holding her for a long moment before lowering her beak and chomping firmly down onto Ellie's arm.

"Ow!"

She jerked her arm down instinctively, which just caused the bird to bite down even harder for balance. Gritting her teeth, Ellie forced herself to walk slowly over to the perch by the window and let the macaw step off onto it.

"What was that for?" she asked, her voice sharper than she would have liked as she examined her arm. "Are you still mad that we moved your cage back in here?"

She sighed. At least Marlowe hadn't broken the skin on her arm, though she was sure there would be a big beak-shaped bruise in the morning. Her feelings were hurt more than anything. It had been a long time since the parrot had tried to bite her. She'd thought they were over that. Apparently she just didn't like being alone; Marlowe was almost twenty years old, and very much used to getting her way.

Still hurt, but trying not to show it, Ellie walked over to the desk and pulled open one of the top drawers, where she kept a small package of unsalted walnuts, one of Marlowe's favorite treats. She opened the package and took out a nut, which she then brought over to the bird.

"Here's a peace offering," she said, holding out the nut. "Life will be back to normal soon enough, I promise."

Marlowe took the nut, turned it over in her beak with her surprisingly dexterous tongue, then with a quick shake of her head, tossed it across the room where it tumbled under a bookshelf.

"What on earth has gotten into you?" Ellie sighed. "We're going to get mice now, unless I can find that nut."

She grabbed her phone off of the desk and turned on the flashlight app as she walked over to the bookshelf. Getting down on her hands and knees, she looked underneath. She saw a lot of dust, some cobwebs, a piece of paper, and way in the back, the walnut. With another sigh, she lay flat on her belly and stretched her arm out as far as she could. Her fingers brushed against the piece of paper and some dust bunnies, but try as she might, she just couldn't reach the nut.

"I'll have to go get the broom later," she muttered. She slid the paper out from under the bookshelf and stood up, still annoyed at the bird's behavior. Bunny, who had finished with her treats, trotted over to see what all of the commotion was about. She stuck her nose under the shelf and sniffed, then blew out breath in a big snort, sending a puff of dust out from underneath.

"It looks like this room could really use a thorough cleaning," Ellie said, chuckling as she watched the dog sneeze, then poke her nose right back under the shelf. "Just one more thing to get to this weekend. Maybe I'll do some upgrades at the same time—the study could use a few basic things like a paper shredder and a new lamp. I swear, Papa kept everything."

She was just about to ball up the paper and toss it in the garbage can as she walked by, when the first line written on it caught her eye and gave her pause. It was a handwritten note, addressed to her grandfather. Instead of throwing it away, she sat down at the desk, smoothed it out, and began reading.

Arthur,

I won't stand for blackmail any longer. I am writing to give you one last chance to stop before I take more drastic measures. We used to be friends, but that won't stop me from doing what it takes to protect myself and everything I have built. Whether you see it or not, I've earned everything that I have. This is your one warning. For your sake, I hope that I never hear from you again.

-T

Ellie reread the note twice, trying to make sense of the words. Her grandfather had been blackmailing someone? It didn't seem possible. Everything she remembered from her childhood, and everything that anyone had ever said about him indicated that Arthur Pacelli had been a good man.

"This can't be real," she said aloud, turning the paper over. There was nothing else written on it, not even a date. How old was the note? Her grandparents had lived in this house for over fifty years. Who knew how long it had been sitting under that bookshelf? It could be decades old... or only a few months old. For a fleeting second she wondered if the note had something to do with her grandfather's death, then she immediately dismissed the theory. He had died of a heart attack in this very office. There had been nothing suspicious about it.

Her first impulse was to show her grandmother. Nonna might be able to shed some light on the issue; she might even know who "T" was. But as Ellie read through the note again, she got an odd, sour

31

feeling in her stomach. What if Nonna didn't know anything about it? Did she really want to risk wrecking the good memories her grandmother had of her late husband? Papa was gone; whatever the note was about didn't matter anymore. Maybe it was best to let sleeping dogs lie in this case.

A knock on the door made her jolt in surprise.

"Come on in," she said, quickly moving her laptop so it covered the paper.

"I just wanted to say a quick goodbye," Danny said as he opened the office door. "I've got to take off. Thanks for dinner. Those pizzas were definitely something special."

"I'm glad you could make it," she said, offering him a polite smile.

"Maybe I'll see you at the pizzeria sometime," he said, grinning. "You've got me hooked. I'll never be able to buy from a chain restaurant again."

"That was my devious plan," she said with a chuckle. He turned to go, but Ellie, struck by a sudden idea, stood up and said, "Wait."

He turned, half out the door and looking curious. "What is it?"

"You knew my grandfather pretty well, didn't you?" she asked.

"Pretty well, I suppose," he said with a shrug. "I worked for him for about a decade."

"Do you have any idea who this letter is from?" she asked, pulling the note out and handing it to him before she could change her mind.

He took it, his frown deepening as he read through it.

"I wouldn't even be able to begin to guess," he said at last. "Where did you get this?"

"I found it under that bookshelf, just a few minutes ago. I'm not sure yet if I want to tell Nonna…"

He nodded, understanding. "Do you think it might have been someone he worked with at the paper mill?"

"Maybe. I have no idea how old it is. You knew him better than I did. Did he seem like the sort of man who would blackmail someone?"

"If you had asked me that ten minutes ago, my answer would have been no," he said. "But this… I really don't know what to think of this. Who's 'T'? Your Uncle Toby?"

"I could be, I guess," she said reluctantly. "But he has to have known more than one person whose name begins with the letter 'T'."

"If you want, I can ask around and see if any of my old friends from the mill know if Arthur might have had a falling out with someone whose name starts with 'T'," he said. "It's worth a try, at least. And you could ask people at the pizzeria."

"If you don't mind, I'd be grateful," she said. "Just don't tell anyone why, okay? I don't want to hurt his reputation, and I definitely don't want Nonna catching wind of this."

"I'll be discreet," he promised, handing the note back to her. "I'll let you know as soon as I hear anything. Goodnight, Ellie."

"Goodnight, Danny. And thank you."

With that, he left, and Ellie was once again alone with the mysterious note and the sinking feeling that she might have just unearthed a secret that would have been better off staying buried for a long, long time.

CHAPTER FOUR

The next day, Ellie found herself late to work once again, this time thanks to Darlene cornering her to besiege her with questions about what she had thought of Danny. By the time she managed to slip out the door, she had come to the conclusion that her cousin was trying to play matchmaker.

She got to the pizzeria shortly after it opened to find Clara and Jacob arguing over who would take the first delivery—a three-meat pizza that had been ordered by a customer notorious for not tipping. Neither of them wanted to make the twenty-minute drive out to his house when they knew he wouldn't even tip enough to cover gas.

"Whoever goes gets credited a free pizza," Ellie told them. "I don't see why either of you are complaining. It's a nice day, and you still get paid your hourly wages while you make the drive. Isn't that better than sitting around in a hot kitchen for the next forty minutes?"

The two employees traded a glance, both of them looking a bit embarrassed.

"Sorry, Ms. Pacelli. I'll go," Clara said, reaching for her keys. "My car is better on gas anyway."

The pizzeria manager turned her head to hide her smile as her employee grabbed the delivery bag and took off, leaving Jacob behind. The young man looked slightly disgruntled.

"Sorry we were arguing," he said. "It's just such a long drive to deliver a pizza to someone who doesn't tip."

"I know," Ellie said. "I don't like it any more than you do when a customer doesn't tip. It's not fair to you guys, but he's still a paying customer, and we have to make sure his pizza gets to him on time. Okay?"

Her employee nodded.

"Shoot," she said suddenly, looking at the clock above the stove. "I need to get a delivery order in by noon."

Feeling harried, she rushed through the kitchen and pushed her way past the doors that led to the dining area. Seating herself behind the register, she wiggled the mouse to turn the computer on and quickly typed in the supplier's website. In the aftermath of finding the note to her grandfather, she had completely forgotten to do the order the night before.

After hurrying through the form and not bothering to double-check her work, Ellie pressed the send button with just a minute to spare. She breathed a sigh of relief. It wouldn't have been fun to have to tell hungry customers that they would have to go without pepperoni, bacon, and sausage on their pizza for a few days because she'd forgotten to order the meat.

Once that was done, she switched with Jacob and let him handle the register while she lost herself in making pizzas. It was easy to get lost in the rhythm of it—spread the sauce, sprinkle the cheese, add the toppings, slide the tray into the oven, and repeat. It was always satisfying to pull a perfectly cooked pizza out, knowing that it would be enjoyed by one of her customers. *I think one of the reasons that I love this job so much is because everything I make brings someone happiness,* she thought. She might not be changing the world, but she was giving people joy all the same—one bite at a time.

She was so lost in her work that the sound of her ringtone startled her and made her drop a dollop of pizza sauce on her apron. Grabbing a paper towel, she did her best to wipe it off as she hurried over to her purse and dug through it with one hand, looking for her phone. When she found it, she glanced at the screen and frowned. It was a local number, but not one that she recognized.

"Hello?"

"Ellie?" a somewhat familiar voice asked.

"Yes, who is this?"

"It's Danny. Darlene gave me your number. Sorry, I didn't know how else to get in touch with you."

"That's fine. What's going on?" Her heart rate increased. "Did you find out something about my grandfather?"

"I think so. But I'd rather tell you in person. Can you meet me somewhere? I'm on my way to Kittiport now, but I've got to be back in Benton Harbor in under an hour."

"Um..." Ellie glanced around the kitchen. Clara had just left on another delivery, and Jacob was about to go out on one himself, but once one of them returned, then the two employees should be able to handle the place just fine. Could she really drop everything and leave like this? Well, she *was* the boss, after all. She might as well use that to her advantage in a situation like this. "I can leave in about ten or fifteen minutes. There's a little diner attached to a gas station right outside of town, on Cormorant Street. We can meet there if you want. It should be quicker for you."

"I know the place. See you soon," he said, then hung up.

Ellie was deep in conversation with one of her customers when Clara got back, then had to run to the restroom before leaving. She winced when she looked at the clock when she was ready to leave at last. She was later than she had meant to be, and hoped that it wouldn't make Danny late for his appointment in Benton Harbor.

"I shouldn't be too long," she told her employee. "Call me if anything comes up that you can't handle."

The diner was only a few minutes away, but the drive felt like it took far longer. She was anxious to hear what Danny had to say, but was also dreading it. Would whatever he was about to reveal change her opinion about her grandfather? Was it possible that he hadn't been such a good man after all? The thought made her feel ill. Her grandmother would be crushed to find out that Arthur Pacelli had kept secrets from her.

There were only a couple of cars in the diner's parking lot when she pulled in. Belatedly, she realized that she didn't know what sort of vehicle Danny drove, and had no way to tell if he was even here yet. She was just about to park and go in when she spotted a white car sitting alone at the far end of the lot. There was someone sitting in the driver's seat, a shadowy form that she was prepared to bet was Danny.

She drove her car over and pulled it up beside to the white vehicle. The person in the car next to hers was definitely Danny—she recognized his haircut. He was sitting slouched in his seat with his head drooping down, sleeping. She felt a momentary pang of guilt. Had he stayed up late trying to find out who the note was from for her? It had probably been unfair of her to bring him into the mystery. He wasn't much more than a stranger, after all.

She got out of her car and walked around to the driver's side of his vehicle, stepping around a pool of some sort of liquid on the ground before rapping on the car's window. Danny didn't respond. She knocked harder, but he still didn't so much as twitch. After only a moment of hesitation, she reached for the door handle, concerned that he would miss whatever it was that he had to get back to Benton Harbor for if he kept sleeping.

"Danny?" she said hesitantly. He still wasn't moving. There was some sort of stain on his shirt... something dark red. Her breath caught in her throat. "Danny?" This time it came out as a whisper. She put a hand on his shoulder and gave him a gentle shake. His head lolled toward her, and what she saw made her stumble back, a strangled scream ripping itself from her throat. There was a matted, bloody wound on the side of his skull, and his eyes were open and staring, but not seeing. Danny Kork was dead.

CHAPTER FIVE

Ellie leaned against her car, shivering from both shock and cold, as she watched Sheriff Ward examine the crime scene inside the car. He was bent over, his head inside the vehicle, being careful not to brush against anything that could possibly be evidence. His deputy, Liam, was busy taking pictures of the area around the car, including the puddle of liquid that Ellie had almost stepped in, which turned out to be blood. The body—she refused to think of it as *Danny*— had already been taken away.

"Did you touch anything other than the door handle?" Russell suddenly called to her across the dead man's car.

"I rapped on the window," she said. "And I touched his shoulder. Other than that, no."

"Did you find something?" Liam asked, looking up with curiosity from his camera.

"Bloody fingerprints just inside the door," the sheriff said. "Make sure you point them out to forensics. I think it's about time I go with Ms. Pacelli to the station. We've made her wait long enough."

His deputy nodded. "I'll take care of everything."

Sheriff Ward straightened up and stepped around the pool of blood outside the vehicle with a grimace. He joined Ellie by her car, his eyes on her face as he tried to gauge how she was feeling.

"Are you ready to go, Ms. Pacelli?" he asked her. She nodded mutely. She was more than ready to leave this rundown parking lot and get out of this clammy weather. "Do you want to follow me, or shall I give you a ride?"

He was looking at her with some concern, and she realized that he was asking her if she was safe to drive. "I'm okay," she said. Her voice came out hoarsely, so she cleared her throat before adding, "I'll follow you."

As they pulled out of the parking lot, Ellie realized that alone in the car with her thoughts might not have been the best place for her to be. She couldn't get her earlier conversation with Danny out of her head. Whoever had killed him would have had only minutes to do it—barely half an hour had passed between when she spoke to him on the phone and when she arrived at the diner. It seemed surreal to think that less than two hours ago, he had been alive and well. Now he was just gone. A terrible thought surfaced. What was she going to tell Darlene?

The drive to the sheriff's department and subsequent walk to Sheriff Ward's office all happened in a blur. Before she knew it, she found herself sitting silently across from him while he typed something into his decade-old computer.

"Can I get you anything to drink before we begin?" he asked her after a moment.

"No thanks," she said. "Go ahead. I'm ready to answer your questions."

"Well, let's start with how well you knew the deceased," he said. "He's a family friend, you said?"

She nodded. "I didn't know him very well. He came over for dinner last night. I have some family from Virginia visiting, and he was an old friend of my cousin's."

"Does he have any enemies that you know of? Anyone who would want to hurt him?"

"I don't know. I barely knew him."

Their conversation continued like that for a while; he asked her questions that she just didn't have the answers to, or had nothing but unhelpful answers to. It wasn't until they reached the subject of why exactly she had been meeting him at the diner that things began to get more interesting. Though she would have rather kept it a secret, she knew that she had no choice but to show him the note that she had found under the bookshelf in her grandfather's study. He read through it with interest.

"So the two of you were meeting because he had some information about who your grandfather was blackmailing?" he asked.

"Yes. But he wanted to tell me in person." She winced. "I'm the one who suggested the diner, because it's right outside of town and he'd be able to get back to Benton Harbor quickly. If it wasn't for me, he might still be alive."

"Why do you say that?" he asked, his steely eyes meeting hers curiously.

"Well, if we had met somewhere else, he wouldn't have been in that parking lot at the wrong time, would he?" she said.

"Hmm." He put the note down. "So you think his death was random, and not related to this letter at all?"

"Well, I—" She blinked. That Danny had been killed because of what she had asked him to do hadn't occurred to her. "If he was killed because he was asking questions about my grandfather, then that means it's even more my fault." Tears began to well in her eyes.

"I'm sorry, Ms. Pacelli, I wasn't trying to upset you." He pushed a box of tissues toward her, accidentally knocking one of the picture frames on his desk over with his elbow as he did. Ellie glanced down to see a photo of a younger version of him with his arm around a gorgeous red-haired woman. They were standing on the beach, both of them smiling broadly.

"Is that your wife?" she asked, dabbing at her eyes, glad for the distraction. A beat of silence followed, and she suddenly remembered that Shannon, Russell's sister-in-law, had told her that he was single.

"Yes," he said shortly, picking up the picture frame and setting it upright again. "She passed away five years ago."

"Oh... I'm so sorry," she said. She felt terrible. How had she managed to cause even more suffering today?

"It's fine." He gazed at the picture for a long moment. "She was murdered. We never found the killer."

Ellie didn't know what to say to this. Saying sorry again wouldn't have covered it, not even close. *It does explain some things about him,* she thought. *Like why he's so obsessed with his work.*

"Anyway," he said, clearing his throat. "I think we've covered all we can for today. I'll be in touch if we need to ask you anything else. You still have my card?" He paused and she nodded. She had put all of his contact information on her phone weeks ago. "Good. If you remember anything or find out anything else about who might have written this letter to your grandfather, give me a call immediately. I'm going to do everything in my power to get justice for Danny Kork."

CHAPTER SIX

Telling Darlene about what had happened to Danny was even harder than Ellie imagined. She had never been good at being the bearer of bad news, and what had happened to her cousin's lifelong friend was worse than any news that she had ever had to break to someone before. She drove aimlessly for a long time before going home, trying to screw up her courage and figure out what, exactly, she was going to say.

Her news was met by stunned silence. The entire family—Nonna, Uncle Toby, Aunt Kathy, and Darlene—was seated in the living room, staring up at her in shock. Unable to look at their faces, she glanced instead toward Bunny. Even the dog seemed subdued; her normally perked ears were down flat against her head, and she didn't so much as twitch her tail when her owner looked at her.

"This can't be real," Darlene said at last, her voice breaking on the last word. She began crying, and the papillon hurried over to try and comfort her. Ellie closed her eyes, overcome with emotion herself. Underneath the grief, guilt niggled at her. She hadn't mentioned her true reason for meeting Danny at the diner, nor the photocopy of the letter to her grandfather that was currently in her purse—Russell had kept the original. Keeping secrets from her family wasn't the right thing to do, but she knew that revealing the letter would just make everything worse.

The next few days were hard on everybody. The Pacelli house was unusually quiet and glum, and even Ellie's work at the pizzeria began to suffer. When she burnt her third pizza in a row the next Tuesday, Ellie threw down her oven mitts, yanked off her apron, and swept her purse off the counter.

"I'm leaving early," she announced to her employees before pushing her way through the staff door in the back and heading toward her car.

Driving aimlessly through town didn't accomplish anything other than serving to help her focus. Her guilt over Danny's death hadn't receded at all over the previous days; if anything, it had grown. She was certain that Danny would still be alive if it wasn't for her. If she had never found that letter under the bookshelf, or if she had just crumpled it up and thrown it away instead of reading it, none of this would have happened. She was responsible for his death just as surely as if she had been the one to hit him on the head.

What made the guilt even worse was the incessant, nagging curiosity. What *had* he found out about her grandfather? What secret could have been grave enough to drive someone to murder to stop it from getting out? She kept telling herself that it didn't matter; a man was dead, and that was a lot more important than anything Arthur Pacelli might have been doing. She had to wipe the letter from her mind; there would be no solving the mystery now, anyway, and it was disrespectful to Danny to keep dwelling on it.

Is it, though? she wondered as she followed the road up the coast. *He died finding out who wrote my grandfather that letter. Wouldn't it be wrong to let everything he did go to waste? Besides, if I find out who was accusing Papa of blackmail, chances are I also find out who killed Danny.*

That thought was a revelation to her, and her mind cleared more than it had been in days. She knew what she had to do. Driving around moping wasn't helping anyone, but digging through her grandfather's past just might lead her straight to the killer.

Ellie had no idea where to start looking herself, but she knew just who would. Her friend Shannon Ward was a journalist, and never turned down the chance to tear apart a mystery. The only problem was, she was married to the sheriff's brother, and she told James just about everything. The pizzeria manager had a gut feeling that if Russell got wind of what she was doing, he wouldn't be too happy, and she wouldn't blame him—he had already rescued her from a bad situation once, and had been first on the scene the time that she had gotten herself tied up and almost shot by a crazed killer. She didn't exactly have the best reputation for keeping her nose out of trouble. Ellie wanted to ask her friend for help, but first had to know whether or not the journalist would be willing to keep a secret.

The answer turned out to be a resounding yes.

"It's not like we'd be doing anything wrong," her friend said, her eyes sparkling at the thought of a mystery to solve. "You're just digging into your family's past, right?"

"Right." Ellie took a sip of her caramel coconut mocha. They were sitting in a tiny café with a view of the harbor. It was only a few buildings down from the sheriff's department.

"I mean, I'm not going to lie to James if he asks me directly, but I can't imagine he would," Shannon continued. "I agree with you that it's probably better that Russell doesn't know that we're looking into this. I love the guy, but he can be a bit overbearing at times. I'm just glad I married the easygoing one."

Ellie chuckled. It was true that the two brothers couldn't be more different, but she wasn't exactly sure she would consider James easygoing, not after watching him single-handedly save all three of them from certain death only weeks ago.

"So, where do you want to start?" her friend asked.

"I was hoping you would have an idea," she admitted.

"Well, what exactly do you want to look for first?"

"I guess I just want to see if there are any news articles or reports about him that might tip me off to who wrote him the letter. He ran the paper mill for years, so there must be *something* about him."

"We can do that. And we're looking for someone whose name starts with a 'T'? First or last name?" the journalist asked.

The pizzeria manager blinked. She hadn't thought of that. She had just assumed that whoever had signed the note had used the initial from their first name. It could just as easily have been from their last name.

"I don't know," she said. "Either, I suppose."

"So we're going to look through old newspaper articles for someone with a first or last name that starts with the letter 'T'—assuming the author of the note wasn't using some sort of nickname, of course— who might have had some sort of contact with your grandfather, and then, if we find something, figure out why your grandfather was blackmailing him or her?"

"That's about it," Ellie said, feeling embarrassed. What had she been thinking? This would be like looking for a needle in a haystack. No, it would be like looking for a specific needle in a pile of needles. Nearly impossible.

"Sounds like fun," Shannon said with a grin.

CHAPTER SEVEN

They spent the rest of the evening in the library going through archived newspaper articles. Ellie was hit with the enormity of their project when Shannon pointed out that Arthur Pacelli had lived in Kittiport his entire life, other than for the years he was at college. Assuming that he didn't meet 'T' until he returned home from the university, that still left them almost sixty years of articles to go through.

The two women sat side by side, scanning through articles for any mention of the name "Arthur," or "Pacelli," until the library began to close. They promised to meet again next time they both were free to continue their search, but despite her friend's support, Ellie walked out of the building feeling defeated. *What did I expect?* she wondered. *Whatever happened between my grandfather and the person he was supposedly blackmailing probably never made it into the papers.* Still, she was resolved to keep searching; at the very least, it gave her something to do, and anything was better than feeling useless.

On her way home, she stopped to check on the pizzeria. Rose and Clara seemed to have everything under control, but she still apologized for leaving so suddenly earlier.

"It's fine, Ms. Pacelli," Rose said. "It's really messed up that that guy you knew was killed. I'd be upset too, if it happened to someone I knew."

"Well, thanks for understanding. It hasn't been easy, that's for sure." She sighed, and decided to change the subject. "How did we do on sales today?"

"Not bad, though we did have one guy order a pizza and never show up to get it. Do you want to take it home? It's a supreme, and neither Clara nor I likes peppers."

"Sure. It'll save me from figuring out dinner," Ellie said, grateful for the turn in luck. She tried not to eat pizza at home more often than she had to, since she had it almost every day at the pizzeria anyway, but she wasn't in the mood to cook tonight. She was more than happy to grab the pizza box and head home, and hope that somehow tomorrow would be a better day.

She parked her car beside Darlene's and sat outside for a moment, not yet ready to go in and face the glum silence that she knew she would find inside the house. To delay going in for as long as she could, she decided to trudge back down the driveway and check the mail, which was delivered in the evenings. Her grandmother was in the habit of waiting until morning to get it, which drove Ellie, who always wanted to see what was in it immediately, crazy.

She opened the mailbox, and sure enough there was a stack of mail still inside. She took it out and flipped idly through it as she walked back toward the house. Plenty of bills, some advertisements; nothing she was particularly interested in. It wasn't until she reached the last item that she paused, coming to a halt in the middle of the driveway. It was a piece of paper, folded up and taped, but not in an envelope, with her name scribbled on the front in pen. Frowning, she slit the tape with her thumbnail and opened it.

> *What happened to your friend will happen to you, too, if you continue searching for the truth. This is your only warning.*
>
> *—T*

Ellie's fingers started shaking, and she nearly dropped the note. Clutching it more tightly in one hand, she used the other hand to dig around in her purse until she found her phone. It took her more than one try to pull up Russell Ward's name in her contacts list, but when she finally got it, she didn't hesitate to press the call button.

She waited for him on the porch, Bunny leashed and at her side. Still reluctant to involve her family more than she had to—increasingly, she was beginning to be concerned for their safety if they learned about the blackmail—after calling the sheriff, she had stepped indoors only long enough to tell her family that she was taking the dog for a walk before leaving again, the papillon in tow. It was another half-truth that she felt guilty about, but she told herself it was for their safety. She didn't want to risk dragging any of them into something dangerous.

Russell parked behind her car, and she hurried to meet him before he could slam his door shut. She thrust the note into his hands, wanting nothing more to do with it.

"I'll have a specialist analyze the handwriting," he told her after reading it through.

"You don't think it's from the same person?" she asked, shocked.

"Of course I do, but an evaluation from a handwriting analyst is more likely to hold up in court than a hunch from the sheriff," he pointed out gently. "Besides, an analyst may be able to pick up nuances in the handwriting that could tell whether the two letters were written within a short time span of each other or not. Handwriting changes as a person ages."

Ellie realized that this could possibly give her a clue as to when the first letter was written. If Sheriff Ward would be able to share any of that information with her, that was.

"Oh. I had no idea." She hesitated, glancing back at the house where three generations of her family sat. "Do... do you think we're in danger here?"

The sheriff considered this question carefully, looking first down at the letter, then at her. When he spoke, it wasn't to answer her question, but to ask one of his own.

"Do you plan on heeding this warning?"

She hesitated, thinking back to her and Shannon's investigation in the library less than an hour before. He seemed to take her silence as a no.

"Then yes, Ms. Pacelli. I do think you are in danger. It's safe to assume that this person has already killed once, and he or she may just be desperate enough to do it again."

CHAPTER EIGHT

When Ellie took Bunny outside the next morning, she was comforted by the sight of a police cruiser driving by. She waved, and the person inside waved back before speeding up and heading down the road. Sheriff Ward had told her that he would schedule extra patrols by her house, and she was glad to see that he was already keeping his promise.

The note in her mailbox the day before had struck a chord deep inside her. Before finding it, she had never even considered that she might be in danger, or that what she was doing might put her family in danger. *Well, it's not like this person would have any way to know what Shannon and I were doing at the library*, she reasoned. Whoever left the letter was probably clueless about that. Danny must have mentioned her name when he was asking questions, that's all. *As long as I don't go around asking the same questions, I should be okay… right?*

Still, she was happy for the visible presence of the deputies. She hoped that they would continue driving by her house throughout the day, but she wasn't particularly worried about her nonna, not with her other relatives in the house as well. There was safety in numbers, after all.

Once Bunny was done with her business, the two of them went back inside and Ellie headed to the study to give Marlowe her breakfast. On her way out, she bumped into Darlene.

"I was just coming to find you," her cousin said. She was twisting her wedding ring around her finger, something that Ellie had noticed that she was prone to doing when she was feeling emotional.

"What is it?" she asked, concerned.

"Since they're still investigating his death, Danny can't have a funeral yet, but his mother is giving a memorial service this morning. I want to go… and I was wondering if you would go with me," Darlene said.

"Of course. When is it?"

"It starts at nine-thirty," her cousin said.

That would give her just under an hour to get ready, but it should leave plenty of time for her to get to the pizzeria before opening.

The last thing she wanted to do was spend the morning in a room filled with Danny's grieving relatives—she already felt guilty enough for his death, and knew that she was likely to burst into tears at the memorial service—but felt that she owed it to him and to his family to go.

"I'll drive," she offered. "Just let me go get dressed first."

It was a grey, dreary day with intermittent sprinkles, as if even the weather was grieving Danny Kork's death. The two women drove through town in silence, Ellie lost in her thoughts, most of which involved wishing she could go back in time. She wished that she had never told Danny about the letter. Better yet, she wished that she had never found the letter in the first place. She didn't want memories of her grandfather to be marred by the accusation of blackmail. Why, oh why hadn't she just crumpled the paper up and tossed it in the garbage? Danny would still be alive, and she wouldn't have the slightest inkling about Arthur Pacelli's shady history.

The memorial service was being held at a church in Benton Harbor. When Ellie and Darlene pulled in, the parking lot was already well over half full. Once they parked, they followed the flow of people inside, though they hardly needed the guidance; the correct room was clearly marked, and just outside the door was a picture of Danny standing in front of what Ellie assumed was his shoe shop. Next to his picture was a framed article that read, *Local Shopkeeper Brutally Killed*. They walked past it, through the door, and joined the people milling around the room.

It didn't take long before Ellie found herself at the table up front where, instead of a casket, a variety of memorabilia was laid out. More photos of Danny, from grainy photos of him as a baby to more recent, modern photos.

"Look, that's us," Darlene said, pointing at an old photo of a boy and a girl about ten years old. Behind them was a sign that said *Pine Cliffs Summer Camp*.

"Darlene?" a voice from behind them said. Ellie and her cousin both turned around. A woman who looked to be in her late sixties or early seventies was standing a few feet away. She was wearing an ankle-length black dress and her eyes were red-rimmed from crying.

"Mrs. Kork?" Darlene said. "I'm so sorry about Danny."

The other woman nodded gratefully, though she was probably used to hearing condolences about her son by then. "I don't imagine I'll ever get used to it. No parent should have to bury their child. Part of me is glad my husband didn't have to go through this."

There was an awkward moment of silence, with Ellie and Darlene both at a loss for words, and Danny's mother gazing past them with a lost look in her eyes. The pizzeria manager watched her, wondering if Mrs. Kork knew that she, Ellie, had been the one to find Danny's body. She definitely wasn't eager to point out that fact if the older woman wasn't aware of it.

"Pardon me, are you Nancy Kork?" an elderly man asked, joining their small group. A younger man was at his elbow, looking uncomfortably around, obviously out of his element at such a formal occasion.

"Yes, I am," Danny's mother said, turning to look at them. "How may I help you? Did you know my son?"

"As a matter of fact, I did," the elderly man said. Ellie judged that he was about the age her grandfather would have been—in his mid-eighties. He leaned on a cane for support, and the young man next to him held on to his elbow for good measure. "Danny used to work under me at the mill. He was a great addition to our workforce. Could really have gone far—in fact, we offered him a management job shortly before he left. I suppose it turned out that he made the right choice when he turned it down. The mill closed down just a few years later."

"I know he was always grateful for that job. It was his first real job, you know. It means so much to me that you remember him so clearly, Mr....?"

"Jack Evedale," he said. "And this is my assistant, Terry."

"Nice to meet you," said the older woman reflexively. "And thank you. It's touching to know that my son made such an impression on you that you remember him even after so many years."

"He was a special young man," Jack Evedale agreed. "I'm sorry for your loss, Mrs. Kork. We can only wish that things had been different."

The pizzeria manager, who had been listening intently to the conversation, felt a tug at her sleeve. She turned to face Darlene.

"People are beginning to sit down," her cousin said in a low voice. "I think we should join them."

Ellie looked around and found that nearly half of the seats had been filled already. She followed Darlene to an empty row near the back and sat down, her mind all the while on the conversation that she had been listening to. Was it possible that Terry was the "T" from the letter? It seemed like a reach, considering that he was so young.

What on earth would her grandfather have been able to blackmail a man barely out of his teens about?

CHAPTER NINE

After the memorial service, Ellie had just enough time to drop Darlene off at the house before hurrying to the pizzeria. Jacob and Clara had already begun the process of opening, but at least she had arrived in time to help. She always felt bad when she didn't do an equal amount of work around the pizzeria, though she knew that her employees probably preferred it when she wasn't there and breathing down their necks the whole time.

"Here's my idea for next week's special, Ms. Pacelli," Clara said once Papa Pacelli's was ready to open. "It's an autumn garden vegetable pizza, with squash and mushrooms and a few other seasonal vegetables."

Ellie took the recipe from her employee and smiled. The pizza looked promising. She would be able to get a lot of the ingredients at local farmer's markets—she knew her customers cared about supporting local businesses—and she was positive that this seasonal pizza would be a hit.

"Looks good, Clara. I'll pick up some ingredients before the weekend. Can you make a sample pizza and take a picture of it for the menu?"

"Yep! I'm glad you like it." She wrinkled her nose. "Clayton kept saying that squash shouldn't go on pizza. But I think it will be good."

Clayton was the young woman's boyfriend; he worked for a cold storage delivery company, and delivered their weekly supply of cheese.

"We'll be sure to give him a slice next time he drops off his delivery," Ellie said. "I'm sure he'll change his mind once he tastes it. Men can be stubborn, but it's usually pretty easy to win them over with food."

"I've noticed," her employee said, laughing. "Oh, that reminds me. Can I have the weekend after next off? He invited me to some family cookout thing at his uncle's cabin in Canada. I know I'm supposed to ask two weeks in advance, but I just found out yesterday."

"I'll have to take a look at the schedule…" the pizzeria manager began. When Clara's face fell, Ellie sighed. "You know what, go ahead. We'll figure something out." She gave the young woman a smile, but mentally winced. She knew that she had probably just committed herself to working extra that weekend.

I really need to hire another couple of employees, she thought. *There are only four of us working here right now. We're managing it, but it doesn't exactly leave any room for emergencies or vacations.* She knew that they couldn't keep this up forever. Short term, her employees might appreciate the longer hours, or rather, the paychecks that came with them. Long term, it would begin to wear thin. The problem was, she didn't have the faintest idea where to start in a search for responsible new employees. Should she post an ad in the newspaper? Or maybe the internet would be better. She shook her head. It was a problem for another day. She had enough on her plate right now without adding a new employee to the mix.

"Ms. Pacelli, you've got people here to see you!"

Ellie jolted, nearly knocking the bowl of pizza sauce next to her hand over. She kept telling Jacob to come and get her if one of the customers wanted to speak to her directly, not shout it through the door. It was unprofessional, and it always made her jump.

Annoyed, she put down the spoon that she had been using to spread sauce over the crust and hurried over to the sink to wash her hands. Then she forced herself to take a deep breath and smile. It wasn't the customer's fault that Jacob had startled her, and most of the time when someone asked to see her personally it was to tell her how good the pizza was, or to ask her a question about bulk orders for events. Whatever it was this time, she didn't want to scare them away with a scowl.

Instead of a happy customer, she was surprised to hear her aunt, uncle, and cousin all standing at the counter. Nonna was conspicuously missing, and Ellie's first thought was that something bad had happened to her grandmother. Then she noticed the smiles on all three faces.

"Surprise!" said Aunt Kathy. "Ma is at water aerobics, so we thought we'd surprise you with a visit before we go pick her up. Do you have time to eat lunch with us?"

Ellie hesitated, then gave them a genuine smile. She wasn't usually a fan of surprises, but this was a nice one. All three of them lived out of state now; the older couple in Florida to take care of Uncle Toby's ailing father, and Darlene in Virginia with her husband. There was no telling when she would see them again after they left.

"Sure," she said. "What sort of pizza would you like? I can go throw it in the oven, then join you. Sit wherever you want."

"How about barbecue chicken?" Uncle Toby asked. "It's been a while since I've had a good barbecue chicken pizza." The two women shrugged.

"Sounds fine to me," Darlene said. She still seemed subdued, and Ellie felt a surge of guilt once again. Danny's death was her fault, whatever way she looked at it. How could her cousin ever forgive her?

"One barbecue pizza coming up," Ellie said in her cheeriest voice. "I'll go put it in now. It should be about a fifteen-minute wait. Feel free to grab whatever you want out of the drink fridge. Lunch is on me."

The pizza was a success, and Ellie couldn't help but smile between bites as she watched her family members dig in. She had gone with thin crust, figuring that would go over best with Darlene and Aunt Kathy, both of whom had grown up eating her grandfather's thin-crust pizza. With just the right amount of sweet barbecue sauce, a gooey layer of Gouda cheese, red onions, and generous amounts of shredded chicken, even she had to admit that the pizza was darn near perfect, though she usually preferred the more classical red sauce variety—on a deep-dish crust, of course.

"I'm glad you don't have any restaurants down in Virginia," her cousin said after her third slice. Ellie raised an eyebrow, and Darlene grinned. "Paul loves pizza, and yours really is some of the best I've ever tasted. If there were a Papa Pacelli's near us, I don't think I'd ever be able to convince him to bring anything else home for dinner."

"I hope he can come with you next time you visit," Ellie said. She hadn't heard much about her cousin's husband yet, but got the feeling that he was busy with work more often than Darlene would have liked.

"I'll see if we can schedule something early next year. Maybe he can take some time off around Easter. He's only ever been to Maine once. I'd love—"

"Watch it!" Uncle Toby shouted, cutting her off. Ellie jumped and turned to see a terrified-looking Clara standing at his elbow. Toby's bottle of soda was on the floor, spilling its fizzy brown contents across the wood.

"I'm sorry," Clara said, clapping her hands to her mouth. "I was just coming to see if you needed anything."

"You smashed into my elbow on purpose," Ellie's uncle said, his voice loud. "Get me a new soda. And clean up that mess!"

Ellie gazed at her uncle in shock. His face was beet red, and he was glaring daggers at her employee. She stood up, sliding out of the booth and putting a comforting hand on Clara's shoulder.

"Don't worry, I'll take care of it," she told the young woman. "I know it wasn't your fault. Go ahead and take a break if you'd like. I've got this."

Clara safely out of the way, Ellie hurried toward the cleaning cupboard, still shocked by her uncle's reaction and fuming at how he had treated her employee. Should she say something to him? Or would it be better just to keep her mouth shut until the older man was out of her hair?

"We'll schedule an appointment with your therapist when we get back," her aunt was saying quietly to her husband when the pizzeria manager returned, mop in hand. "You haven't had an outburst like that in a while. Have you been doing your breathing exercises, dear?"

"Yes, I have, Kathy. This is not my fault!" her uncle said grumpily. "That girl should have been watching where she was going, clumsy fool."

Ellie kept her mouth shut as she mopped up the mess, but her mind was racing a million miles an hour. Did Uncle Toby have an anger problem? She remembered Danny asking if the "T" from the letter to her grandfather could have been her uncle. At the time, she had dismissed the thought, but now she wasn't so sure that had been smart. If her uncle had issues with anger, then maybe he had done something in a fit of rage… something bad enough that her grandfather could have used it for blackmail.

CHAPTER TEN

Even after her family left, Ellie wasn't able to shake the anxious feeling that had started when her uncle went off on Clara. The rest of the meal had been eaten in a frigid silence. Their goodbyes had been short and clipped, and the pizzeria manager was still toying with the idea of saying something to him when she got back to the house this evening. She did not want *anyone* to treat her employees poorly, let alone her own family.

Yet, despite her anger, she kept her mouth shut even after getting home. A long walk with Bunny helped, mainly because by the time she got back she was too cold to think of anything but taking a warm bath. Thankfully, the bathroom that she was currently sharing with Darlene was unoccupied, and she was able to take a relaxing soak for as long as she wanted. She heard the rise and fall of voices downstairs, but was glad that she couldn't make out what they were saying. She didn't need any more stress for the day, and found herself even more eager than before for her extended family to leave. *Just a few more days*, she thought. *Then there will be peace and quiet around here again. Not to mention, the bathroom will stop looking like a hurricane went through it every morning.*

After her bath, she retired to bed early, still not sure what she was going to say to her uncle, and deciding to leave it until morning. She expected sleep to come quickly after the busy, emotionally upsetting day, but it remained elusive. She just couldn't stop thinking of her uncle's angry outburst today, and her mind kept flashing back to Danny asking if the letter could have been from Tony. It was possible, of that she had no doubt… but judging from what she had seen today, her uncle wouldn't exactly be open to answering questions about his past. She would have to do some digging on her own.

With a sigh, Ellie gave up on sleep and got out of bed, doing her best to be quiet. Bunny, who had been dozing on the pillow next to her head, woke up and gave her a confused look, obviously wondering what her person was doing up at such an odd hour.

"Shh," the pizzeria manager said, holding a finger to her lips. "I'm going to the basement. Want to come with me?"

The dog stretched lazily, then hopped off the bed, gave herself a good shake, and looked eagerly at the door, ready for whatever adventure they were about to embark on. Ellie smiled, grateful as always for the papillon's companionship. At least she wouldn't be *completely* alone while she dug through her grandfather's old things in the basement, though she doubted that the dog would be much help when it came to defending her owner against spiders and other nasty things.

"We have to be quiet," she whispered as she opened her bedroom door. "We don't want to wake anyone."

She made her way slowly down the stairs, wincing each time a step creaked. After a quick stop in the kitchen to grab a flashlight from one of the drawers, she opened the basement doorway and urged Bunny down the steps. The little dog hesitated, knowing that she wasn't usually allowed down there, but with some more urging finally began making her cautious way down. Ellie followed, closing the door behind her and sealing them both in utter darkness. She flicked on the flashlight and followed the dog to the bottom of the stairs.

"All right," she said in a whisper. "Let's get to work."

One of the first things that she had done after moving in and taking over the study was to move the bulk of her grandfather's files into storage in the basement. She had gone through them first, reading through anything that was relevant to the pizzeria, but the old man had kept records of *everything*, and the bulk of it she had overlooked, since it had nothing to do with Papa Pacelli's. Now she was hoping that he had something about his son-in-law buried somewhere in all of the papers. Or failing that, something incriminating about someone else who had a name that began with "T." Whether or not finding the person that had written the letter solved Danny's death, she was determined to find out just what had driven Arthur Pacelli to blackmail someone.

It took her hours, sitting on the basement floor on top of an old, musty wool blanket with Bunny curled up next to her thigh and papers spread out across her legs, to find what she was looking for. It was in a file folder dated three years before she was born—so over forty years ago. The label on it said simply *T.D.* Toby Dirschell. Feeling wide awake, Ellie opened it and shone the flashlight on the papers inside. The first thing she noticed was a picture of a young man who looked to be in his twenties; presumably, the younger version of her Uncle Toby. The photo was paper clipped to an article with the headline; *Road Rage Leads to Fatal Crash.*

Ellie read through the article with bated breath. Sure enough, it was about her uncle; the story alleged that her uncle had driven a middle-aged man off the road. The incident, the reporter said, likely happened when the victim tried to pass young Toby on a two-lane country road. Toby had sped up, not letting the driver change lanes even when a truck came from the other way. The man attempting to pass had been forced off the road to avoid a collision with a truck, and had smashed full-speed into a tree instead.

It was a chilling article. Ellie turned the clipping over, hoping for more, but there was nothing else in the file except for a short note written in what she recognized as her grandfather's hand.

> *My dear daughter,*
> *I know you don't wish to hear from me on this subject again, but even though it will make you angry with me, I feel that you must know the truth—*

The next sentence was scribbled out, and the note was left unfinished. Ellie stared at it for a long time, wondering what it meant. Had her grandfather ever finished another version of the letter and sent it, or had he decided not to interfere with his daughter's love life? Had he held the incident over Uncle Toby all these years, threatening to tell his daughter that he had been responsible for a man's death? Was this what her grandfather had been blackmailing him about? Did it prove that Uncle Toby was the "T" from the letter to her grandfather?

There were too many questions, and not nearly enough answers. Ellie let the file folder fall shut and stood up, wincing at the tingling as blood rushed back into her legs. It looked like it was time to start asking her family some questions. First thing in the morning, she was going to confront her uncle.

CHAPTER ELEVEN

Confronting her uncle was a lot easier resolved than done. When she woke up in the morning, she had a sick, anxious feeling in the pit of her stomach. She kept glancing toward the file, wondering if she could really trust a decision made by her sleep-deprived brain the night before. She wanted to get to the bottom of the mystery, she knew that much, but she wasn't quite sure how to begin. Somehow, it didn't seem like a good idea to walk downstairs and accuse her uncle—a man that she knew had anger issues—of murder. Then again, she could only beat around the bush so much before he realized something was up. Was it better to be direct? Should she maybe ask her aunt, first? What would she say? *Good morning, Aunt Kathy. Would you like some coffee? By the way, is your husband a killer?*

She snorted, waking Bunny up, which settled one thing for her; whether or not she was going to speak to her uncle this morning, she couldn't spend any more time in bed. The papillon was making it clear that she had to go out, and she had to go out *now.*

"You were asleep two seconds ago," Ellie grumbled good-naturedly as she grabbed the file from her nightstand. "You can't suddenly have to go potty *that* badly."

It was a clear morning, but uncomfortably cold. She shifted on her feet, watching as the black-and-white dog zig-zagged across the yard with her nose to the ground, following the trail of some critter or another that had wandered across the grass during the night. Covering her mouth as she yawned, Ellie was surprised to hear the screen door slide open behind her.

"Hey," Darlene said softly, joining her on the porch.

"Hey," she replied. "You're up early. How are you doing?"

Her cousin shrugged. "It hasn't been easy. But I didn't come out here to talk about Danny. I wanted to apologize."

"For what?"

"For my dad." Darlene frowned. "It's been a while since I've seen him have an outburst like that. This whole thing must be stressing him out. I think he gets confused sometimes. He doesn't want to admit it. He says sixty-one is too young for his mind to start going. I know mom is worried about him."

"I don't really know what to say," Ellie admitted. "The way he spoke to Clara... well, it was unacceptable. I'm grateful that you apologized to me, but really, he should be the one apologizing, and to her."

"I know," her cousin said with a sigh. "I'll talk to him about it." Her eyes drifted down to the file folder, which was still in Ellie's hand. "What's that?"

The pizzeria manager hesitated. The night before, she had vowed to confront her uncle. In the morning light, after a night's rest, the thought was intimidating. Could her cousin possibly help? She decided to take a chance.

"Darlene," she said, taking a deep breath, "let's go to the study. We have a lot to talk about."

With Marlowe watching them from her wooden perch by the window, a piece of one of Nonna's famous blueberry muffins clutched in her claws, Ellie told Darlene everything. She showed her the letter that she had found under the bookshelf the week before, and explained that she suspected Danny's queries about it had played a role in his death. She also let her cousin read the article about Toby, and explained her suspicions. She tried to be as thorough as she could, and was grateful that the other woman didn't interrupt her with questions.

When she fell silent at last and Darlene still didn't say anything, she began to get worried. It was impossible to tell what her cousin was thinking. She must be shocked, but other than that… was she upset? Hurt by the secrets her family had kept? Or had none if it even registered with her yet? Ellie knew it could be a lot to take in.

"I can't believe you," the other woman said at last raising her head and meeting Ellie's eyes. The pizzeria manager was shocked to see fierce anger on her cousin's face. "Danny died because of you. And now you have the gall to try to drag my father into this?"

"Darlene—" Ellie began.

"I don't want to hear it." Her cousin blew out a slow breath. "I need to be alone right now, before I say something that I really regret. Just know this, Ellie… I may not be able to change the fact that you're my cousin, but after this, you will never be my friend."

With that the other woman stood up and stalked out of the study, leaving Ellie at her desk, stunned and hurt.

Upset beyond words, she called the one person that she knew she could count on to support her. Half an hour later, she found herself in a coffee shop with her best friend, feeling significantly less upset and even more intrigued by the mystery of Uncle Toby and her grandfather. All of that was thanks to Shannon, who had read through the article about the road rage incident as if she was starving for information.

"Ellie," she said once she had finished the article. "You're brilliant. Have you told Russell any of this yet?"

"Not yet," the pizzeria manager admitted. "Do you think I should?"

"Well, I don't think it's enough for him to connect your uncle to the murder, not unless he has strong evidence that the killer was the same person that wrote the note, but he might at least be able to question the man."

"Do you think my uncle killed Danny?" Ellie asked, feeling suddenly doubtful. Was she just grasping at straws?

Shannon considered her question for a moment. "If he was the one your grandfather was blackmailing, then I think it's definitely possible," she said at last. "Keeping his past a secret from your family could definitely be a motive for murder. If he somehow found out that Danny was asking around about it, maybe he got paranoid and snapped. He could have easily left that letter in your mailbox, too."

"You're right," Ellie said with a shiver. The fact that she had been sleeping under the same roof as a potential killer for the past week and a half was suddenly starting to feel very real. Were any of them safe? "I should get home. I need to see if I can calm Darlene down, and then call the sheriff. Thanks for your help, Shannon."

"You don't have to thank me. This is the sort of thing that I live for." Her friend grinned, then more seriously added, "Be careful, Ellie. From everything you've told me, this uncle of yours could be dangerous. I don't want you to get hurt."

CHAPTER TWELVE

Ellie spent the drive back to her house planning out her apology to Darlene. She just hoped that her cousin hadn't said anything to Uncle Toby yet. The last thing she wanted was for the older man to know what she knew. Shannon was right; he could be dangerous. It was very possible that he had already killed, not once, but twice if she counted the road rage incident. She really didn't want to become the third victim.

She had prepared herself for all manner of welcomes when she got back, from stony silence to anger. What she hadn't been expecting was an empty driveway. Both Darlene's and Nonna's cars were gone. Ellie stared at the empty spaces for a moment, wondering if something terrible had happened, when she remembered with a guilty jolt that they had planned to visit her grandfather's grave this morning.

Promising herself that she would make it up later by buying him an extra nice bouquet of flowers, she switched her engine off and went inside. She doubted that she had time to join them—they were probably on their way back already. She might as well just begin getting ready for work.

"Bunny," she called out. "I'm home. Where are you?"

Her puzzlement quickly turned to concern when the little dog failed to come running. The papillon *always* greeted her at the door.

"Bunny?" she called again, her heart beginning to pound. Only something serious would keep the dog from her. She thought back through the morning. Had she somehow left Bunny outside? No, she was certain the dog had followed her and Darlene into the study. *The study! I must have locked her in there accidentally when I left,* she thought with relief.

She hurried down the hall and opened the study door, and gasped in shock at what she saw. The desk drawers were pulled open and there were papers everywhere. Her laptop was open, the lock screen informing her that the incorrect password had been entered too many times and she would need to confirm her identity via email to access the computer again.

"Bunny?" Ellie whispered, her first crazy thought that the dog had somehow caused this mess. But no, that was impossible. The little, seven-pound papillon wouldn't have been able to open the desk drawers, let alone her computer. Her eyes shot toward the bird cage, the macaw her next suspect. The cage, however, was securely shut, and Marlowe was huddled in the corner, looking terrified.

Someone had broken into the study and ransacked it. Even worse; her dog was still missing.

She rushed through the house, checking behind every closed door in the faint hope that the papillon had somehow gotten herself locked away. When she headed into the kitchen with the desperate idea to check the pantry in case Bunny had slipped inside without notice, she stopped in her tracks. The kitchen door was wide open, letting an icy breeze and a few stray leaves inside. Bunny wasn't in the house anymore; of that, she was certain.

After twenty minutes of fruitless searching outside, Ellie realized that she had no choice but to call the police. They might not just come out for a missing dog, but they certainly would when she told them that her house had been broken into.

It didn't take long for the sheriff's truck to arrive. Ellie was waiting anxiously outside, keeping her eyes peeled in case Bunny was close by. The dog couldn't have gotten far, not as tiny as she was. A hundred yards would be like a mile to her.

She was relieved to see Russell. While she liked both of his deputies, Bethany was young and inexperienced, and she simply didn't know Liam that well. She knew that the sheriff would take her seriously, and hoped that he might even be willing to help her search for Bunny after he had taken her statement.

"Who else has a key?" he asked. They were standing by the back door, already having examined the study. Ellie, who hadn't done much more than glance at the mess before, had forced herself to slow down and do a quick inventory while the sheriff waited. Nothing had been missing, which he had dutifully noted down on his notepad when she told him.

"My grandmother," she said. "That's it."

"And you're sure you didn't leave it unlocked when you left earlier?" He crouched down to examine the door frame.

"I don't think I did," she said, trying to think back. "I've always locked it before." This time she had been distracted by Darlene though, hadn't she?

"Well, it doesn't look like it was forced," he said, straightening up.

"We have guests staying here. Family," she explained. "They left after I did. It's possible that one of them left it unlocked."

He nodded. "And you're positive nothing was taken from your home office?"

"I'm pretty sure," she said. "If anything *was* taken, it wasn't anything valuable, or anything that I would notice."

"Whoever broke in left your laptop and an expensive animal," he mused. "This doesn't look like a robbery. Can you think of any reason one of your family members might have gone through your office?"

Ellie opened her mouth to say no, she couldn't, but stopped herself. She thought of the file folder with the article about Toby that was currently sitting in the passenger seat of her car, and the photocopy of the letter to her grandfather in her purse. She remembered the sound of Darlene slamming the door behind her as she stormed out. Had she told her father about Ellie's suspicions? There were plenty of reasons that Darlene or Toby would want to go through her office; one of them had probably been looking for the file.

"I think," the sheriff said, watching her expression, "that you have a lot that you had better tell me. Shall we walk and talk at the same time?" He gestured to the door.

"Huh?" she gave him a puzzled look.

"You want to find your dog, don't you? I can help you look while you tell me what's been going on around here."

A wave of gratitude washed through her. "Yes, of course. Thank you. I'll tell you everything—I was going to, anyway, before I came home to all of this."

She took a moment to organize her thoughts as they walked toward the woods, and started speaking just as they stepped beneath the boughs, pausing every few minutes to call out Bunny's name and listen for the jingle of her collar before continuing with her story.

CHAPTER THIRTEEN

She had just finished telling Sheriff Ward everything that had happened since they had last spoken when she heard a familiar jingle up ahead. Ignoring the spiky branches catching on her pants, she pushed forward to find a very dirty, cold, and scared Bunny huddled between two fallen branches. She scooped the dog up and was rewarded with a flurry of warm kisses across her cheeks. The little papillon's tail was wagging so quickly that it was nearly invisible.

"Oh my goodness, Bunny, don't ever do that again," Ellie said, hugging the dog close. "What would have happened if we didn't find you?"

She was embarrassed to feel tears prick the corners of her eyes. Bunny was her constant companion, and she would be completely crushed if something had happened to her, but that didn't mean that she wanted to cry in front of the sheriff. She sniffed quickly, hoping he would think that she was getting a cold, and gave the dog a quick once-over.

"I don't think she's hurt," she said, turning back to Sheriff Ward. "Thank you so much for helping me find her."

"My pleasure," he said. "I'm glad she's okay."

She fell into step beside him, trusting him to know the way back through the forest. "What are you going to do about Toby?"

He glanced sideways at her. "Nothing."

Ellie blinked. "What… what do you mean, nothing?"

"I have absolutely nothing to connect him to Danny's murder," he pointed out. "An old newspaper article about him driving someone off the road in a fit of rage hardly ties him to the case I'm investigating now."

She opened and closed her mouth, feeling like an idiot. He wasn't even going to talk to Uncle Toby?

"But he's leaving in two days," she said. "If I'm right and he *is* the one that killed Danny, then he's just going to get away with it."

"I'll do what I can to speed the investigation up," he told her. "But these things take time, and I have to go by the book. If I don't, the whole case could get thrown out—even if he *is* guilty."

They walked in silence the rest of the way back, Ellie carrying her dog and thinking about what the sheriff had said. She knew that he was right. There really wasn't anything at all connecting Toby to Danny's murder. That meant that she was just going to have to try harder to uncover the truth before he left.

When they reached the house, she was shocked to find her aunt, uncle, and grandmother all waiting on the back porch. She had completely forgotten that they would be back soon. What must they have thought when they returned home to find the sheriff's truck in the driveway and they house completely empty?

"Ellie, I was so worried," Nonna said, hurrying forward as best she could to give her granddaughter a hug. "I thought something terrible had happened."

"I'm fine," the pizzeria manager assured the elderly woman. "Don't worry, no one's hurt and nothing's missing… but someone did break into the house."

All three of them gasped. Ellie searched her uncle's face, looking for any sign of guilt. Did he know? Had Darlene told him? Was he the one that had ransacked her office? She looked around, suddenly realizing that her cousin was missing.

"Where's Darlene?" she asked.

"She's staying with a friend," Kathy said, sighing. "She seemed upset, but she wouldn't tell me much. I think Danny's passing really got to her. She'll be glad to get home at the end of the week, I'm sure."

"Oh." Ellie felt a pang of guilt. Had she really managed to drive her own cousin away?

"Ellie dear," her grandmother began. "Aren't you supposed to be at work?"

"What time is... Shoot!" Ellie handed the papillon off to her grandmother. According to her phone, it was half past twelve. The pizzeria had long since opened, and she hadn't so much as called to let her employees know that she would be late. She glanced down at her clothes and bit back a curse when she saw that she was covered with mud and leaves. Leaving Russell to take statements from her family members and trusting that Nonna would get Bunny cleaned up, Ellie hurried upstairs to change before heading in to work.

The good thing about being the boss was that she couldn't get fired for being late. If she could, she reflected, she would have long since been let go. At least her employees knew their way around the pizzeria and could handle pretty much anything the day threw at them without her input.

Papa Pacelli's was unusually busy when she walked in. Both Rose and Clara were in the kitchen, which wasn't normal; only one employee was usually needed in the kitchen at a time. They both seemed relieved to see her, which she also found odd. She didn't think that any of her employees particularly disliked her, but she never got the feeling that they particularly enjoyed having her there either.

"We've got a big party eating in," Rose explained as she hurried past with a plastic bin full of shredded cheese. "I think it's one of their birthdays."

Curious, Ellie put her purse and jacket away and stepped through the kitchen doors to the dining area. Sure enough, a large group of college-age young men were sitting in the corner. They had pulled a couple of tables up to a booth, making enough room for all of them. She was surprised to find that she recognized one of them; Terry, the old man's assistant from the memorial service. He met her gaze, and she was certain that he recognized her, too. She gave him a small wave, feeling a bit bad for ever having suspected him as Danny's murderer. He looked younger than ever now; he couldn't have been much more than a year or two out of high school.

As they served the party pizza after pizza, Ellie had to admit that she was glad it wasn't this busy every day. They would need more ovens if it was. It seemed like ages before the party finally got up to leave. The pizzeria manager breathed a quiet sigh of relief at the register as she watched them begin to walk out the door in ones and twos. She was surprised when Terry walked over to the register.

"I'm sorry about your friend," he said in a low voice with a nervous glance over his shoulder, as if worried that his friends were going to leave without him.

"Thanks, Terry," she said, giving him a small smile. "You have a nice day."

He hesitated. "You, too," he said after a moment before turning around and hurrying to join his group.

It's too bad he already has a job, Ellie thought as she watched them leave. *I really could use a nice kid like him here at the pizzeria.*

CHAPTER FOURTEEN

A soft whine sounded next to Ellie's ear. She turned her head to the side, struggling to hold on to sleep. Only when something cold and wet touched her face did she open her eyes.

"What is it, Bunny?" she muttered. "Do you have to go out?"

The dog whined again, a soft whimpering sound that Ellie hadn't heard her make before. She sat up, reaching for the bedside lamp as she glanced at the clock. It was slightly past midnight.

"Are you okay?"

She turned to look at her dog in the light, wondering if she had somehow missed an injury during her cursory examination after she found the papillon in the woods. Seeing that she was finally awake, the dog jumped off the bed and began scratching at the bedroom door. *Maybe she ate something that didn't agree with her while she was outside,* the pizzeria manager thought. Not wanting Bunny to

109

have an accident, she hurriedly pulled her slippers on and ushered the dog through the door.

Instead of running to the back door, the papillon surprised her by heading instead to the living room. Ellie paused just beyond the door. A soft glow was coming from within. Was someone in there? Not sure what to expect, she braced herself and rounded the corner. Her grandmother was sitting on the couch, and Bunny was perched on the cushion next to her, head on her leg.

"Oh, Ellie, I'm sorry if I woke you," Nonna said. She wiped a hand across her face, and Ellie realized that she must have been crying. She looked down and saw a photo album in her grandmother's lap.

"It's all right, Nonna. What's wrong?" She sat down on the couch on the other side of Bunny, concerned for the elderly lady.

"I just miss him," she said, gazing down at the photo album. Ellie recognized her grandfather in some of the pictures. "I know we were lucky to get as many years together as we did, but I was hoping for so many more. I know we were both getting up there in age, but still… his death was so sudden."

Ellie froze. She had never really heard much about her grandfather's death before, and had never asked about it, not wanting to make things harder for her grandmother. She wondered, for the second time, if the person who had written her grandfather that note had somehow also been responsible for his death.

"He didn't... have any heart problems or anything?" she asked tentatively.

"He had high cholesterol, but he took medicine for it," Nonna said. She heaved a tremulous sigh and shut the photo album. "It must have been his time to go, that's all." She gave a faint smile. "Did I ever tell you about the night that he passed away?"

Her granddaughter shook her head.

"I woke up in the middle of the night, certain that I had heard a man's voice," Nonna said. "Art wasn't next to me, which wasn't too unusual. He wasn't a very deep sleeper, and suffered from insomnia for the last few years. Anyway, as I lay awake, waiting for him to come back to bed, I could swear I heard that voice again. I wondered if Art was on the phone, and decided to go and see who it was." She took a deep breath. "But when I got to his study, I found him already gone. I'm convinced that the voice I heard was his spirit, telling me goodbye for the last time."

Tears filled her grandmother's eyes again, and Bunny snuggled closer to her, doing her best to comfort the old woman. Instead of sorrow at her grandmother's story, Ellie felt as if her veins had suddenly filled with ice.

That voice hadn't been her grandfather's ghost saying one last goodbye to his wife. No, someone else must have been in the study with him. And that meant her grandfather must have been murdered.

After walking her grandmother back to her bedroom, Ellie took Bunny upstairs and sat down on her bed. After a moment's thought, she stood up, locked her bedroom door, and sat back down again. What was she going to do? This wasn't just about Danny anymore. Someone had killed her grandfather, too. And if her hunch was right, that someone was snoring not too far away from her at this very instant. How could she be expected to spend the night in the same house as Uncle Toby, let alone the next two days? Surely this counted as proof, didn't it? Would the sheriff be able to do anything?

She glanced at the clock, her fear battling with her desire not to be rude. It was past midnight. She should probably wait until morning to call Sheriff Ward. On the other hand, he might be upset if she knew where a killer was, but waited hours to report it. She bit her lip, torn with indecision. At last, fear won out. She wouldn't be able to stand staying in the house with Uncle Toby all night; her nerves were already frayed as it was. The sooner he got arrested, the better, as far as she was concerned.

Picking up her cell phone, Ellie scrolled through her contacts until she found his personal number. She hit the call button and put the phone to her ear, hoping against hope that he was still awake.

"Hello?" a sleepy voice answered. She winced. He definitely hadn't been awake.

"Hi, Sheriff Ward," she said, keeping her voice quiet. "It's Eleanora Pacelli."

"Pacelli?" There was a rustling sound, and she imagined him sitting up in bed. He sounded more awake when he spoke again. "What is it?"

"My grandfather was murdered," she said. "My uncle did it. I have proof."

At his request, she relayed the conversation that she had had with her grandmother only minutes before to him. He didn't seem quite as impressed with the information as she had imagined.

"What's your proof?" he asked when she had finished.

"I just told you," she hissed. "My grandmother heard voices the night that he died. He can't have been alone. Someone must have been in the study with him. Someone killed him!"

"Ms. Pacelli, when I ask for proof, I'm looking for something solid. Fingerprints. A bloodstain. Maybe some nice photographic evidence. A voice heard in the middle of the night by a woman well into her eighties is hardly incriminating. Did she hear what the voice said? Was the person speaking having a conversation?"

"I don't think she could make out what they were saying, no," Ellie said. "And she only ever said that there was one voice. A man."

She could hear him take a deep breath over the phone. "And did it occur to you that this mysterious voice could simply have been a dying man trying to call out for help?"

Ellie fell silent, her cheeks flaming with embarrassment. He was right, and she knew it. She had jumped the gun on this one. There was still nothing to tie Toby to either crime, and she had just woken Kittiport's sheriff in the middle of the night for nothing.

"I'm sorry," she said, defeated. "I shouldn't have called. But Uncle Toby is guilty, I just know it. Everything fits—he would have been able to put the letter in the mailbox without anyone noticing, and he would have had ample time to go through my study, even with the other women in the house. No one would have noticed; I'm usually the only one that goes in there." Something else occurred to her, and she sat up straighter. "And Marlowe—the parrot—she *hates* him. She won't stop screaming while he's around. My grandfather kept her in his study; if someone had killed him, she would have witnessed it."

"You're telling me that your bird witnessed a murder, understood what had happened, and still hates the person responsible months later?"

"Macaws are very smart and have terrific memories," she said. "I think she would have realized what was going on."

He made a sound somewhere between a groan and a chuckle. "You are very determined, aren't you?"

"I don't want to see a murderer walk free," she said. "Do you?"

"I can't do anything without some sort of evidence," he told her again. "I can't arrest a man with no connection to the murder scene and no motive beyond the contents a mysterious note that he might or might not have written. Everything you've told me is speculation. I'm not saying I don't believe you—I'm not necessarily saying that I do, either—but I definitely can't act on it."

"Can't you bring him in for questioning?"

"I could question him about Danny's death. That would be reasonable, considering that the victim had dinner with your family the night before he died. I don't know if that would do much good, though. I wouldn't legally be able to hold him, and if he is guilty, it might put him on his guard."

"What if," Ellie began, her mind racing, "you could question him while he was off guard, relaxed, and slightly drunk?"

"What are you talking about?"

"We're having a dinner tomorrow night—it's supposed to be the big goodbye dinner before they leave. Nonna's making lobster, and there will be wine and beer. He almost always has something to drink with dinner, and he tends to get kind of loud. You could ask him questions, try to get him to confess something incriminating, and if he does, arrest him on the spot."

"That could be considered entrapment," he said. "I like the way you're thinking, but we've got to keep this by the books. And he wouldn't be at all suspicious that the sheriff just happens to be having dinner with you?" Russell asked, sounding amused. Ellie guessed that he was thinking that she was getting ahead of herself again, but this time she had a plan. She grinned.

"Not if you're my date. Is it entrapment if you come over for dinner and just happen to hear something that incriminates him?"

"No," he said after a pause. "I guess not." She couldn't tell from his voice what he was thinking. Had she convinced him?

"Sheriff Ward, will you be my date to dinner tomorrow night?" she asked, reflecting that this was the first time that she had asked out a man since before she had started dating Kenneth. It was almost a pity that it was for a fake date.

"Oh, all right," he said. "I'll be there. But you'd better start calling me Russell."

CHAPTER FIFTEEN

Ellie spent most of the next day avoiding her uncle as much as she could. She took Nonna shopping with her, unwilling to leave the defenseless old woman at home with a killer, and when they returned laden with groceries, she volunteered to put them away on her own. The question of how to broach the subject of her bringing a date to dinner was nagging at her. Darlene had made it clear through a series of text messages that she would not be joining them for dinner, though she had promised to pick her parents up early the next morning for their trip back down to Virginia. No one was in a particularly good mood—by then it was obvious that *something* had happened between Ellie and her cousin, though it seemed that no one knew for sure what, and she was more than happy to keep it that way.

Finally, she caught Nonna alone and broached the subject of Sheriff Ward coming to dinner—or Russell, as she had to remember to call him.

"I think that's wonderful, dear," her grandmother said with a genuine smile. "I'm so happy that you're starting to be comfortable with dating again."

That left Ellie feeling worse than ever. She hadn't told an outright lie, but she had definitely misled her grandmother into thinking that she was romantically involved with someone. *After all of this is over, I'll tell her everything,* she promised herself. *No more sneaking around.*

She was relieved when it was time to start making dinner. Uncle Toby, who had no interest in cooking, was in the living room watching television, leaving the three women in the kitchen together. Aunt Kathy and Nonna tried to keep things fun and lighthearted, but Darlene's absence was conspicuous and brought them all down. For her part, Ellie was just counting down the minutes until Sheriff Ward arrived. She was positive that nothing bad would happen with him around. And if it did, well, he would be able to take care of it. It was doubly comforting to know that regardless of what happened tonight, by this time tomorrow, she would no longer be sleeping with a murderer in her home.

When the doorbell rang at last, Ellie rushed to answer it. She smiled at the sheriff, noting that he had dressed up for the occasion. She had only ever seen him in his uniform, or in his fishing gear, and he cleaned up nicely. She realized for the first time that pretending that he was her date had the potential to be more than a bit awkward. *We're just doing this to catch a killer*, she reminded herself. *At the very least, I highly doubt that Uncle Toby will try anything with him here.*

"Come on in," she said, giving him a smile. "Dinner is nearly ready."

"It smells great," he said. "Did you cook?"

"I helped. My grandmother was the mastermind. She has a way with lobster. I was on pasta duty."

"Sounds like a family effort," he said. He followed her indoors, then crouched down to greet Bunny, who seemed to have taken a liking to him. Probably, Ellie figured, because he had had a hand in saving her not once, but twice.

There were an awkward few minutes while they sat in the living room with her aunt and uncle, until at last Nonna announced that they could sit down. They were eating in the formal dining room, not the cozy breakfast nook in the kitchen where Ellie was used to taking her meals. The table was large enough to seat twice their number comfortably, and once again she was struck by the absence of Darlene. She was surprised that her cousin was missing this. Her theories must have really upset her cousin when they'd argued.

Despite the thousand worries that were weighing her down, Ellie couldn't help but notice that the meal was absolutely delicious. The lobster was cooked to perfection, and even the pasta she'd made had turned out better than she expected. She had been afraid that the alfredo sauce would be her stumbling point, but it was actually some of the best that she had ever tasted: smooth, creamy, and the perfect accompaniment to the lobster tail. The salad was her aunt's invention. Kale, arugula, and a variety of other dark greens dressed with a champagne vinaigrette made a refreshing side to the heavier flavors of the main course. A bottle of her grandmother's favorite chardonnay sat on the table, and Ellie watched eagerly as her uncle poured his first glass.

"Wonderful meal, ladies," he said, raising his glass in a toast.

"I just wish Darlene was here to enjoy it," Kathy replied with a sigh.

Uncle Toby's brow furrowed, and he shot Ellie a look. She still didn't know for sure if he knew what had gone on between the two women, but if he did then he was the world's best actor, because he had been acting just as confused and curious as everyone else.

"So how long have to two of you been seeing each other?" her aunt asked, clearing her throat and turning her attention to Russell.

"Not very long," he replied with a glance at Ellie. "We first met a couple of months ago."

"Well, I hope you have many more happy months together," Kathy replied with a smile. "We all know her history. She could do with a good, sensible man in her life."

Ellie coughed, frantically searching around for a new subject to bring up. "Aunt Kathy, how do you like Florida? What's it like this time of year? I've never been there."

"Oh, it's very humid, and the summer is relentlessly hot. I have to say, I don't miss the snow, though, and the Everglades are just beautiful."

"I don't like it much myself," her uncle said. "It's too touristy. I keep trying to convince Dad to leave his house and move somewhere else, but he refuses. That in-home care of his is costing him a pretty penny, that's for sure."

"Oh, you don't live around here?" Russell asked, raising an eyebrow. "How long have you been out of state?"

"Three... no, four years," Kathy told him.

"When did you last visit?"

"I made it up for Pa's funeral," she told him. "Toby couldn't. His father had just had surgery, and he wanted to stay close."

"When's the last time you managed to get up here?" Russell said, turning to Toby. Ellie watched the exchange, wondering what the sheriff was getting at.

"I haven't," Toby said matter of factly. "Not since we moved."

Russell took another serving of lobster and shot Ellie a meaningful glance. She pondered everything that had been said, trying to figure out the significance. When it struck her, she felt like a complete idiot. If Toby had been in Florida for the last four years, then he obviously hadn't been in Maine to kill her grandfather just a few months ago. It didn't clear him of Danny's murder, though. She wondered how to bring up the subject of blackmail naturally, then decided to just go for it. She was just opening her mouth to speak when her phone buzzed in her pocket. Out of habit, she pulled it out and glanced at it, and was shocked to see a text from Darlene.

R u alone?

Ellie glanced around the dinner table. She was far from alone. What on earth did her cousin want?

"Excuse me," she said, pushing away from the table. "I'll be back in a moment."

Taking her phone with her, she made her way to the kitchen and sat down at the breakfast nook.

I am now, she texted back. *What's going on?*

Need u 2 meet me, came the reply.

Where? She asked.

The mill Danny used 2 work at. I know y he died.

Ellie stared at her phone's screen. Darlene was at the paper mill? Had she been investigating Danny's murder the whole time?

Her phone buzzed again. *Come alone.*

Why? She texted back, feeling the first threads of suspicion.

Her phone was silent for a long time. At last it buzzed, and a sinister message popped up on the screen.

Come alone or your cousin dies.

CHAPTER SIXTEEN

Ellie was frozen to her chair. It wasn't Darlene texting her. It was someone else. Someone who had her phone.

"What do I do?" she whispered. She could hear laughter from the other room. It would be so easy to go back in there and get the sheriff. Whoever was texting her would have no idea. Or would they? What if they were watching her? Anyone could be lurking outside, gazing in through the windows. If she brought the sheriff along with her, she might end up getting her cousin killed, and she would never be able to live with herself if that happened.

Knowing that she was making the stupidest decision of her life, Ellie grabbed her purse from the counter and slipped down the hallway, past the dining room, and toward the front door. She paused at the threshold, waiting for some sort of common sense to kick in, but it didn't. She was doing this, and she was doing this alone.

She knew, roughly where the abandoned paper mill was. The drive to it was a dark one, with the moon hidden behind the trees, and left Ellie a lot of time to think. If she wasn't careful, both she and Darlene might very well disappear for good tonight. But how could she save them both, without alerting the person or people that were texting her using her cousin's phone? *How do I even know that Darlene is still alive?* Shaking her head, she forced the thought away. If she thought like that, she would lose her courage before she even got there.

The mill was eerie at night. The stacks were visible before Ellie even turned onto the private drive. She paused at the turn off and pulled her phone out—she had a plan, and she had to put it into action now. Any closer to the mill, and she ran the risk of someone seeing the glow of her phone's screen. Scrolling down her recent calls list, she found the sheriff's number and hit the call button. Turning the speaker volume down as far as it would go, she slipped the phone into her pocket. She could only hope that Russell would answer and keep listening as whatever events were about to happen unfolded. If he let the call go to voicemail, he was going to find one heck of a message waiting for him in the morning.

She turned onto the driveway and drove up it slowly. One light was visible in the mill, oddly bright against the otherwise dark building. Her heart beating harder than ever before, she parked near the first door that her headlights illuminated and shut the engine off. It was nearly impossible to resist the urge to check her phone and see if the call had actually gone through or not, but she knew that anyone looking out from inside the building would easily be able to see her phone's screen light up. The last thing that she wanted was for them to realize that she was calling the police.

Ellie got out of her car and pushed her way through the mill's doors. The interior was dark, and nearly impossible to navigate. She began heading in the direction that she thought the light had come from, only to trip over some sort of metal contraption. Landing on her hands and knees, she gasped in pain.

"This way," a voice said from directly ahead of her. "He wants to talk to you first."

A flashlight clicked on, illuminating her path. She followed the beam, trying to see who its owner was. The male voice was familiar, but she just couldn't place it. *Well, at least I know it isn't Toby,* she thought, wanting to kick herself for every bad decision that she had made over the past week.

"Who are you?" she asked. The person said nothing, just kept leading her through the dark halls with the bright beam of his flashlight. Remembering her plan, Ellie raised her voice slightly and spoke as clearly as possible "Why did you make me come to the paper mill?"

Once again, there was no answer, but Ellie was okay with that. She hadn't been speaking for his benefit anyway, but rather the benefit of the man that she hoped was listening in through her phone. She tried to ignore the fact that she very well might not even have any bars of service out here—the call could have been dropped before it connected.

At last they came to a door with light behind it. The person who was guiding her opened it and stepped through, leaving her to follow. She blinked against the glare—the light was some sort of super-bright industrial lamp—and looked around. Immediately she recognized Terry. She gasped. He had been the one guiding her through the halls.

"It's you," she said, aghast. "You're 'T' after all."

"Huh?" the young man said, looking at her blankly. "I'm Terry. Why'd you call me 'Tea'?"

"She's talking about my letter," a second voice said from behind her. She spun around and found herself face to face with Jack Evedale.

"*Your* letter?" she said. "Why did you sign it with the letter 'T'?"

130

"I'm not going to sign it with my real name, am I?" he said, chuckling. "It stands for my nickname back when Art and I were younger. When I first got into business management, people called me Tiger because I was so driven and brought so many people down on my climb to the top. It stuck."

"I don't understand. How did you know my grandfather?" she asked. "And where's Darlene? You promised she'd be here."

"I promised no such thing," he said coldly. With a chill, she realized that she hadn't even asked him if her cousin was there before rushing out of the house to meet him. "But you're in luck. We kept her alive just in case you decided to ask for some sort of proof." He gestured to the corner, where Darlene sat on the floor, bound and gagged. Ellie made a move toward her, but Terry came up behind her and grabbed her by the shoulder.

"How did you know my grandfather?" she said again, talking to Evedale, but keeping her eyes on her cousin.

"We were friends," the old man said. "He was the general manager here for nearly twenty years. I handled the accounts. We got along famously until he discovered that I had been siphoning money off for years, making myself quite wealthy. He had the nerve to blame me for the mill shutting down and all of the workers losing their jobs."

"So he began blackmailing you? Why didn't he just turn you in?"

At this, Evedale gave a sharp laugh that turned into a cough. "If he reported me, all of the money would just go back to the owners of the company. Instead, he forced me to make payments to the workers that had been laid off, and donations to charities. He did that for twenty years, and was sucking me dry. I'm getting older, and as you can imagine, my medical bills have been racking up. I couldn't afford his charity cases anymore."

"So you killed him," Ellie said flatly.

"No," the old man said with a note of hurt surprise in his voice. "I simply told him how it was. I asked that he stop for the sake of our past friendship. When that didn't work, I sent Terry with another message, this one a bit more intimidating. Terry has a way with locks, you see. Didn't you wonder who broke into your grandmother's house? Anyway, I pointed out that if he turned me in, he would end up guilty too, as an accomplice. He's known about the stolen money all these years, and has done nothing."

"But he died," Ellie said, aghast. "My grandmother said she heard voices that night. You must have been there."

This time it was Terry who answered, surprising her by sounding almost regretful. "The old guy had a heart attack," he said. "I was talking to him, and he just keeled over. I didn't mean to kill him. I don't even know that I did kill him. He might have just... died."

"It was unfortunate," Evedale said, not sounding like he thought it was unfortunate at all. "But it did solve my problems. At least, until Danny boy asked me about the note. I hadn't realized it had been found. I knew then that my troubles were far from over."

Ellie stared at him for a long moment, taking in his frail frame and the cane that he was leaning on. "There's no way you killed Danny," she said. "He would have overpowered you." She realized with a shiver who must have done it; the same man who had killed her grandfather. She twisted out of Terry's grip and took a step backwards, away from both of them.

"I didn't want to," Terry said in a small voice. "I didn't. But he said I was in it too deep, and if he went to jail, then so would I."

"And what about Darlene and me?" Ellie asked, tremulous. "Are you just going to kill us, too? Can you live with that?"

She forced herself to meet Terry's gaze, despite her revulsion toward him, trying to appeal to whatever sense of human decency was left in the young man. He opened his mouth, then hesitated, glancing at the old man beside him.

"Of course he can," Evedale said. "He's a strong boy."

"Killing two women isn't strong. It's cowardly," Ellie countered. "Please, Terry. We never hurt you. Don't listen to him anymore. I'll even testify in court that you saved us. Darlene will too." She glanced toward her cousin in the corner, who nodded, terrified.

"I don't... I don't know..."

"Take out that gun I gave you, boy, and do it!" the old man snapped. "We need time to get rid of the bodies before people start looking for them."

"I don't... Mr. Evedale..." Terry looked frantically between her and his boss, torn.

"Do you remember Danny's memorial service?" Ellie asked desperately. "Do you remember how crushed his mother looked? Can you really do that to our family too, Terry?"

The young man met her gaze, then took a deep breath. "No. Mr. Evedale, I quit."

"You can't quit," the old man snapped. "I have dirt on you. I'll tell the police everything. You'll rot in prison for life."

He began hobbling toward the young man, who looked terrified. Ellie screwed up her courage, took a step forward, and kicked the cane out from Evedale's grip. Evedale stumbled, reaching out to Terry for balance, but his assistant recoiled, letting the old man crash to the floor. Darlene gave a sob of relief as Ellie rushed over to untie her.

EPILOGUE

"I can't believe my plan worked," Ellie said, feeling almost giddy as the realization sunk in that everything was going to be okay. She really had thought that she was going to die for a while there. "I didn't think you would get the call, or if you did, everything you heard would be all garbled since the phone was in my pocket."

"You shouldn't sound so proud of yourself," Russell said. He looked angry, and Ellie decided to avert her gaze and focus intently on the paramedics examining Darlene. "Your plan *didn't* actually work, since we *didn't* get here in time to save you. If Terry hadn't had a change of heart, things would have turned out very differently. You could have gotten yourself and your cousin killed. What you did was dangerous."

"They would have killed her if I had told you anything," she said, lifting her chin slightly, but still refusing to meet his gaze. "They told me to come alone."

"An old man and his twenty-year old assistant? They had no way of knowing what you were doing. You could have called the entire United States Marine Corps, and those two still wouldn't have known a thing until the tanks rolled up to the mill."

"Well I didn't exactly know it was them, did I?" she asked, finally getting upset enough to face his anger head on. "I risked my life for a family member, and I ended up saving her. No matter what you say, you won't be able to convince me that it was the wrong thing to do. I wouldn't have been able to live with myself if she had died, not if it was my fault." She wrapped her arms around herself, realizing for the first time that she had left her jacket at home.

Russell stared at her for a moment, his jaw muscles flexing. At last he sighed, evidently deciding to give up on their argument for the moment. "You're shivering," he said, removing his sports coat with a shrug and handing it to her. "It would be a bit too ironic if you managed to survive this fiasco, only to die of pneumonia a week later."

She was still hurt by his reaction to everything that she had done, but accepted the jacket anyway. She *was* cold.

"I'll admit one thing," she said. "I was wrong about Uncle Toby. I'm sorry. I shouldn't have relied so much on hunches and guesses.

I've learned that there's a good reason to do things your way. It saves you from embarrassing mistakes."

"I've learned something too," he said. She looked up, and was surprised to see his lips twitch up in a smile. "Never trust one of your hunches."

Made in the USA
Middletown, DE
10 December 2016